AFTER DEAD

AFTER DEAD

CHARLAINE HARRIS

ACE BOOKS, NEW YORK

THE BERKLEY PUBLISHING GROUP
Published by the Penguin Group
Penguin Group (USA) LLC
375 Hudson Street, New York, New York 10014

USA • Canada • UK • Ireland • Australia • New Zealand • India • South Africa • China

penguin.com

A Penguin Random House Company

This book is an original publication of The Berkley Publishing Group.

AFTER DEAD

Ace Books are published by The Berkley Publishing Group.
ACE and the "A" design are trademarks of Penguin Group (USA) LLC.

Library of Congress Cataloging-in-Publication Data

Harris, Charlaine.
After dead : what came next in the world of Sookie Stackhouse / Charlaine Harris.—First edition.
pages cm
ISBN 978-0-425-26951-0 (hardback)
1. Stackhouse, Sookie (Fictitious character)—Fiction.   2. Vampires—Fiction.   3. Werewolves—
Fiction.   4. Magic—Fiction.   5. Harris, Charlaine—Characters.   I. Title.
PS3558.A6427A69   2013
813'.54—dc23
2013030521

FIRST EDITION: November 2013

PRINTED IN THE UNITED STATES OF AMERICA

10   9   8   7   6   5   4   3   2   1

Cover, endpaper, and interior illustrations by Lisa Desimini.
Cover design by Judith Lagerman.
Cover photograph of clouds © Elenamiv/Shutterstock.
Interior text design by Kristin del Rosario.
HBO® and True Blood® are service marks of Home Box Office, Inc.

For the grandchildren.
They are our future.

A NOTE FROM THE AUTHOR

After I began writing the final novel in the Sookie Stackhouse series, I was deluged by questions from readers who all wanted to know the same thing: how to find out what happened to a score of characters who couldn't make an appearance in the last book. It was obvious I couldn't fit all of the people in Bon Temps and its environs into *Dead Ever After*. So in the interest of satisfying the readers who've been following Sookie's adventures for years, I herewith present my coda to the books that have dominated my professional life for over a decade.

THE ANCIENT PYTHONESS continues to be cared for by the vampires of Rhodes. The donors from the Donor Bureau who are sent to her have to be carefully briefed, because giving her blood is terrifying and definitely unsexy.

GREG and **CHRISTY AUBERT** continued to work at Greg's insurance agency, Pelican State. Greg, a natural witch, struggled with using his innate power to improve his business after he almost ran all the other insurance agents in Bon Temps into the ground. He underwent an intervention (telling the psychologist he was an alcoholic) to change his behavior. Not too surprisingly, the treatment didn't work very well. Greg finally managed to impress Greg Jr., who was watching from the garage one day when his dad re-inflated a tire by pointing his finger at it. Lindsay, Greg and Christy's daughter, sowed her wild oats and then settled down to teach tap and jazz dancing to little girls in Clarice. She married a farmer.

CONNIE BABCOCK, the deceitful secretary at Herveaux and Son, was not able to get a comparable job after she was fired. She ended up working as a guard at a correctional facility.

DOKE, **MINDY**, **MASON**, and **BONNIE BALLINGER** are living happily in Texas. Doke got laid off for a while, but he was called back to work before things got too tight. Mindy got a job working as a secretary at the high school, and she really enjoyed it. Mason had nightmares about the day of his uncle's wedding, but his parents talked to him a lot and sent him to a counselor, and he got through it. He became a manager at a mattress factory. Bonnie didn't remember that awful day the wedding was picketed by protesters, but she became an activist for various social causes later in life. She was also the best veterinarian in west Texas.

CHRISTIAN BARUCH was accused of unprofessional behavior at a meeting of the Vampire Hoteliers Association. He was never seen again.

BATANYA and **CLOVACHE** are still working for the Britlingen Collective, which continues its business of providing protection in several dimensions to whoever can pay for it. Batanya thinks Clovache is the best partner she's ever had, and they've had many adventures in many strange situations. So far, they've come out alive.

ISABEL BEAUMONT, Dallas vampire, racked up an impressive body count among the rebels responsible for killing her king, Stan. She still lives in Dallas and has become Joseph Velasquez's right hand. She never dates humans.

ALCEE and **BARBARA BECK** went away for a vacation in Hawaii after the events of *Dead Ever After*. They returned after two weeks with some very interesting underwear and big smiles on their faces.

ANDY and **HALLEIGH BELLEFLEUR** welcomed their daughter, Caroline, two months after the events of *Dead Ever After*. Caroline was born with a heart defect, but after some surgery she lived a relatively normal life for many years. They had two more children, sons Jared and Clayton. Caroline's heart defect unexpectedly caused complications when she was a senior in high school, and Andy and Halleigh buried her in her cheerleader uniform. Jared and Clayton both became lawyers like their aunt Portia Bellefleur Vick.

TERRY and **JIMMIE BELLEFLEUR** welcomed many litters of pups to their double-wide, and three of the pups won prizes at Catahoula shows. Eight years after their marriage, the couple died in a two-car accident as they returned from a grandchild's birthday party. Terry was sincerely mourned by Jimmie's children and grandchildren, and they gave a donation to the VA hospital in Shreveport in Terry's honor. It was earmarked for the treatment of prisoners of war.

BELLENOS the elf was glad to return to Faery with Dermot, and they go hunting together often. When Bellenos found a female elf to marry, Dermot gave him a handsome wedding present: a metal relief plaque embellished with the likenesses of the heads of those Bellenos had slain. It has a place of honor above Bellenos's hearth.

BERNARD the vampire, a great friend of Russell Edgington's, became an even better friend of Christopher Hauser, the vampire king of Germany. Bernard was named Christopher's consort. He's unchangingly cute.

POLLY BLYTHE was fired from her position with the Fellowship of the Sun. She found a job as a public relations contact with a Pat Robertson–style ministry but was fired from that, too, after she told a newscaster during an on-air interview that he was bound for Hell. She became a telemarketer.

JANE BODEHOUSE died five years after the end of *Dead Ever After*. She blacked out while she was sitting on the toilet and cracked her head against the edge of her sink. Marvin found her the next day. Marvin Bodehouse never got married, but he also never took a drink.

The vampire short-order cook **ANTHONY BOLIVAR** became a celebrity chef and appeared on the Food Channel several times. After he was arrested for picking up a prostitute and overdrinking from her, the Food Channel asked him to pack his knives. He began traveling again and occasionally takes a night shift at a restaurant . . . maybe one near you.

Lawyer **KATHERINE (KATE) BOOK** is still an undead activist. She has to practice in night court, of course, but she's featured in magazines all the time as a poster woman for all that is good about vampires.

BOOM still works on the bomb squad in Rhodes.

Shut away in Faery forever, **DERMOT BRIGANT** is extremely happy. He basks in his father's affection and has a very uncomplicated sex life. He is spell-free.

DILLON BRIGANT had already disowned his remaining child, Claude, well before Claude escaped from Faery. Dillon spent the next few hundred years keeping a low profile, because he didn't want to remind his father, Niall, that a family member tried to overthrow Niall's government.

NIALL BRIGANT spent a few decades suspecting that there were plots against him behind every door because of Claude's rebellion, and many of the fae suffered for Claude's misbehavior. Every now and then, Niall thought of Sookie and sent her a letter via rosebush.

AMELIA BROADWAY had a son with Bob. After many arguments over what to do with her father's business and money after he was declared legally dead (Bob wanted to give it to charity), the couple split up, but they shared custody of their son, Felix, until he was eighteen. Amelia sold her father's business to a large chain, invested the proceeds, and used her witch skills to play the stock market. She amassed a huge amount of money and married her banker. Felix became an animal wrangler for the film industry, specializing in big cats.

BUBBA continued to be passed from vampire kingdom to vampire kingdom, but while he was in Tennessee, he escaped from his minder to visit his gravesite, causing a near riot. After that, the vampire council censured Tennessee and ruled that Bubba couldn't enter the state for fifty years. He is in Canada now. He hates the winters.

CALLISTO drifted over to the Middle East, where she caused dreadful bloodshed but went unnoticed.

Wright's **PORTER CARPENTER** took special courses to become an expert in crowd control. He got the job of police chief of Arlington, and then he was hired by Fort Worth.

DESMOND CATALIADES remained a friend to Sookie, developing a habit of dropping in before Christmas every year. His children didn't approve of his attachment to a human, but in view of what happened when their father was unhappy, they never spoke to him about it. Mr. Cataliades declared New Orleans a devil-free zone, and he enforces that doctrine vigorously. He continues to practice law.

DIANTHA CATALIADES was a teenager for only ten more years. She still has a startling sense of fashion, and she still works for her uncle. She also has a seasonal job at a fireworks factory.

CHARLES CLAUSEN finally found a nice lady wereowl to nest with.

HANK CLEARWATER contracted gonorrhea.

PARKER COBURN lived with Rubio Hermosa and Palomino for fifty-seven years. After a fight about who had left the bathroom light on, Parker moved to Las Vegas, where he's become a door-opener at a casino owned by Felipe de Castro. He's looking for congenial vampires with whom to nest.

BILL COMPTON developed a warm relationship with Karin the Slaughterer. He built a secret daybed for her on the second floor of the Compton house. Though eventually their physical ardor abated, Bill was glad to have Karin's input when he began creating and producing violent vampire-themed video games. He recruited a stable of young computer-oriented men and women who agreed to work for Bill exclusively for twenty years in exchange for being brought over. Eventually, Bill had to add on to the Compton house to accommodate his nest. He became extremely rich and was featured in all the vampire magazines, and not a few human ones. He strolled across the cemetery to visit with Sookie from time to time. He always loved her. A surprising development was made possible by all the money he earned from his computer empire: see *Felipe de Castro*.

Detective **MIKE COUGHLIN** was shot and killed in the line of duty when the Wendy's where he was having lunch was robbed. Detective **WILLIE CROMWELL** was wounded in the same incident, but he recovered. He had to retire because of his injuries.

ALFRED CUMBERLAND reached the pinnacle of his career when he photographed the marriage of Sheriff Pam to Heidi.

Barmaid **CYNDEE** got another job at another vampire bar in Mississippi after being fired from Fangtasia. But she made the same kind of trouble for a vampire who was less in the public eye than Eric, and she went for an unexpected and fatal swim in the Mississippi.

DEVON DAWN's appearance on *The Best Dressed Vamp* made her an overnight celebrity, but her fifteen minutes of fame was over after a couple of months. She gladly went back to obscurity, though she dressed much better.

BUD and **GRETA DEARBORN** enjoyed their retirement together in the harmony that marked their marriage. Bud had a stroke at seventy-five and never recovered, and three years later, Greta passed away in her sleep. The town renamed a street in Bud's honor, and the memorial scholarship started in Greta's name sent one of Terry Bellefleur's step-grandchildren to college.

King **FELIPE DE CASTRO** reigned over Arkansas, Nevada, and Louisiana for thirty more years. By that time, his kingdom had gotten too complicated and cumbersome for one vampire to run, so he sold Arkansas to his regent, Red Rita, who set up her own kingdom. After an earthquake damaged two of his casinos in Las Vegas, Felipe rebuilt them with the money he got from selling Louisiana . . . to Bill Compton, who makes a great king, though he refuses to move to New Orleans.

MARK DUFFY was struck on the head with a beer bottle in another barroom fight, and he died after two days of insisting he was fine.

Tara's husband **JB DU RONE** kept his job at the health club in Clarice, rising to assistant manager since everyone helped him out. JB was beloved by his twins, who twisted him around their little fingers, and JB was also loved by strong-minded women, who were likewise able to talk JB into permitting liberties he ought not to have permitted. Tara put up with it as long as she could, but eventually she kicked him out. JB continued to have lady friends his whole life, and he married two or three of them (they insisted), but he never had any more children and he never thought of anyone but Tara as his true wife. Still handsome, he passed away in his nursing home while he was having sex with an aide.

ROBERT THORNTON DU RONE and **SARA SOOKIE DU RONE** were read the riot act by their "aunt" Sookie after their second trip to the police station. She described their mother's childhood in frank terms and told them how remarkably lucky they were to have a mom who had overcome such odds, because she would need all that toughness to survive her twins. It was a wake-up call. Rob graduated from Louisiana Tech and began working for a state senator. Eventually, he became a senator himself. Sara got a full scholarship to Tulane and became a speech therapist.

TARA THORNTON DU RONE raised her twins to be good citizens. She had to pick them up at the police station twice. After that, they calmed down. Tara remarried once for about ten minutes. She built up Tara's Togs and did a good amount of Internet business. She moved into the storefront next to hers, and that became Tara's Bridal and Formal Boutique, which eventually became a destination shop for brides in Louisiana. She arranged JB's funeral service and cried a lot.

Vampire **DUSTIN** finally learned the dos and don'ts of being a modern American vampire, and he writes a monthly column for AVO, the website devoted to American Vampires Online.

IMMANUEL EARNEST became the favorite hairdresser of a well-known rock band and toured with them until he went back to L.A. to found his own salon, Night Cuts.

RUSSELL EDGINGTON is still the King of Mississippi. He still likes to be surrounded by comely young men, but then so does his husband, Bartlett Crowe, King of Indiana.

FotS sympathizer **HELEN ELLIS** married another FotS member. Since they were bonded together by mutual hatred, they had a bumpy marriage, and they were terrible parents.

ERIN married Remy Savoy after dating him for a year. She was a loving mother to Hunter and bore Remy a little girl who could never get away with anything, given her half brother's gift of telepathy.

OCTAVIA FANT lived with Louis Chambers in a small house in New Orleans until a tree branch, broken by a violent storm, crashed down on the corner of the roof that covered their bedroom. When Octavia's niece came to clean out the house, she decided to burn all the magic aids and accoutrements that Octavia and Louis had accumulated. Amelia found out too late to rescue it all.

FARRELL still lives in the Dallas nest and still dresses like a cowboy.

HOYT FORTENBERRY married Holly Cleary, who became pregnant on their honeymoon. In addition to stepson Cody, the two raised a son, Jason, and a daughter, Moonlight. Jason Fortenberry married Marie Stackhouse.

MAXINE FORTENBERRY and her silent husband, Ed, lived out their lives happily, taking care of their grandchildren.

Arlene Fowler's children, **COBY** and **LISA FOWLER**, were adopted by Brock and Chessie Johnson. Coby became an independent filmmaker and shot a movie about his mother's death, which won awards but caused a lot of unhappiness in the Bon Temps community. Coby had severe emotional issues for his whole short life: He died of an accidental drug overdose at forty-seven. Lisa became a romance writer, and she married three times.

FREYDA is still the Queen of Oklahoma, and she has never regretted her bargain with Eric.

LUNA GARZA became the face of Latina two-natureds, and she lobbied for the rights of Animal Americans until she was well into her sixties, when she retired to a ranch in New Mexico to paint landscapes.

DANIELLE GRAY lived with a couple of guys but never quite made it to the altar again. Her daughter, Ashley, scored really well on her ACT and got a full ride at a community college. From there, she financed the rest of her college tuition by dancing at a gentlemen's club, and she earned enough to become a nurse. Danielle's son, Mark Robert, worked for Wal-Mart his whole life.

GINJER HART continued to pass bad checks until she spent five years in jail. After that, she reformed her ways. She lectured to high schools and Sunday school classes for a modest fee, and she worked at a thrift store.

Even after **HEIDI**'s addicted son, Charlie, died in an alley within two years of her moving to Louisiana, Heidi stayed in Shreveport. She married Pam. They swap clothes, and every now and then they go hunting for drug dealers. Heidi developed such a good reputation as a tracker that she occasionally helps the police search for missing people and fugitives.

CATFISH HENNESSY continued to be content with watching sports on television, managing the road crews, and going square dancing with his wife.

RUBIO HERMOSA died in a freak construction accident in Baton Rouge, where he'd drifted after his nest broke up.

ALCIDE HERVEAUX finally stopped being foolish and impulsive where women were concerned. When his rogue werewolf lady turned out to be a poor match, he became interested in a surveyor who worked for one of his business rivals, a werelynx named Callie Brown. Callie, a short, compact, no-nonsense kind of woman, kept Alcide in order for the rest of his life. She had five children with Alcide, and she went to work at Herveaux and Son, which after a period of time became Herveaux and Sons when the three boys started work there. Of their two daughters, one became a beauty pageant contestant and eventually Miss Louisiana, and the other became a social worker. Alcide and Callie had fifteen grandchildren. They both passed away at advanced ages.

BRENDA HESTERMAN sold antiques in Shreveport even after the mysterious disappearance of her partner, Donald Callaway. She eventually retired to Florida.

The goblin **MR. HOB** still works at Josephine's (Club Dead) in Jackson, Mississippi.

BARRY (HOROWITZ) BELLBOY spent three weeks with Sam's mom. He never went out after dark. When he was well enough, he got Bernadette to drive him to the airport (DFW), where he rented a car and started driving. He ended up in Seattle. He lay low there for a year or two. We may hear more about the rest of his life.

INDIRA eventually moved to New York to become part of the large Indian American vampire group there. She joined an Indian dance troupe, and they perform at state fairs and Indian weddings.

ISAIAH is still the King of Kentucky.

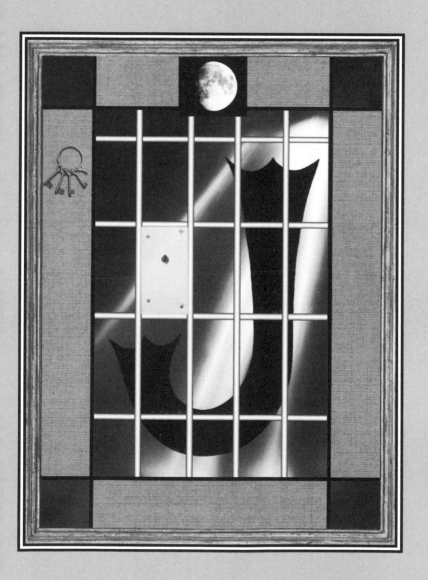

After splitting up with Amelia, **BOB JESSUP** continued to work at the coven's magic shop. The coven put him in charge after five years, and he did a good job. He had a live-in companion for a long time (fellow witch Terencia Rodriguez, who helped Amelia at the ectoplasmic reconstruction), until she died of breast cancer. He was very involved in the life of his son, Felix, and while he admired Amelia's developing business acumen, Bob did not envy her. Bob had a witch funeral arranged by the coven, and it was incredible.

BROCK and **CHESSIE JOHNSON** adopted Coby and Lisa Fowler and raised them with a lot of love and a lot of financial struggle.

KENYA JONES and **KEVIN PRYOR** went to church with wedding rings on one Sunday. Kevin's mother collapsed and said she couldn't breathe, but she recovered when Kenya offered mouth-to-mouth resuscitation. After a year or two, Mrs. Pryor and Kenya learned to tolerate each other, much to Kevin's relief. The couple never had children, but one of Kenya's nephews lived with them until he went to college. They always referred to him as their son.

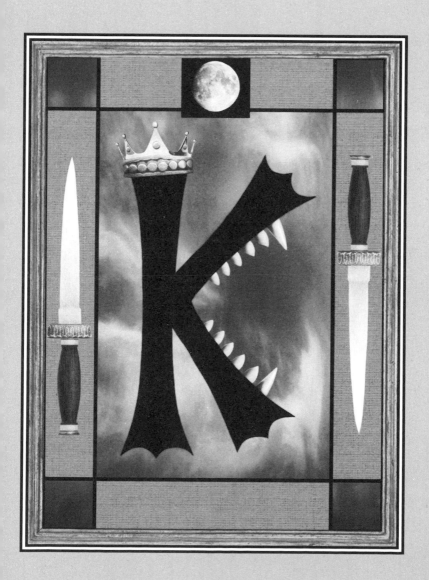

KENNEDY KEYES cohabited with Danny Prideaux for two years, after which their differences drove them apart. Kennedy, no longer as controversial a figure as she had been when she first walked into Merlotte's, found a job at the casino in Shreveport, tending bar in a very abbreviated outfit. She married a businessman twenty years older than her, outlived him easily, and began raising and breeding bulldogs. She married her gardener when she was sixty.

MUSTAPHA KHAN joined the Long Tooth pack and was a member in good standing for forty years. He took a job as Pam Ravenscroft's daytime man, and he also earned a little extra money as a bouncer at the casino. He and Warren stayed together until Mustapha's fatal motorcycle accident on an icy highway.

FBI Special Agent **TOM LATTESTA** had the misfortune to be visiting the BVA in Washington when the FotS made one of its last terroristic statements by bombing the building. He did not survive the explosion.

ANTOINE LEBRUN cooked at Merlotte's for five more years, saving his money carefully. He opened a hamburger place close to the high school and called it the Hawks' Nest. It was instantly successful, because Antoine made the best milkshakes in Bon Temps. He married one of Kenya's sisters.

MAXWELL LEE became the face of vampires in Shreveport, since Pam tended to say exactly what she was thinking, with poor public relations results. The suave Maxwell gradually assumed more and more responsibilities after Bill Compton became king, until he became almost synonymous with Louisiana vampirism. He loves every minute of it, though he'll never admit it.

LAYLA LARUE LEMAY and her maker and lover, Sean, have so far been able to stay together, though child and maker usually can't. They still dance together. They've been invited to work on the vampire version of *Dancing with the Stars*.

BEV LEVETO was cohost of *The Best Dressed Vamp* until its cancellation, when she began to host *America's Top Vampire Model*.

The **LISLE** family remained based in Wright, Texas. Angie, Deidra's younger sister, was so impressed by the power of prayer at Deidra's wedding that she became a Methodist minister. Jared, Deidra's older brother, survived Afghanistan to become career army. Mr. and Mrs. Lisle became friends with Bernie Merlotte and set an example for the community by making it clear she was welcome in their home. Mr. and Mrs. Lisle had several grandchildren. They urged all of them to elope.

DR. AMY LUDWIG went public with her clinic for the treatment of supernaturals. She has a huge problem with addicts breaking in to steal the exotic drugs they're sure she keeps around. She's hired the twin Weres Dixie and Dixon Mayhew to guard the clinic at night. Sometimes they're in wolf form when they're on the job. Problem solved.

DAHLIA LYNLEY-CHIVERS still lives in Rhodes and continues to have her own adventures.

MCKENNA took over the everyday wear shop, Tara's Togs, when Tara du Rone opened the wedding boutique next door. McKenna eventually married a cousin of Glen Vick's.

SISTER MENDOZA married her patrol partner, Tony Gonzales. They remained in Wright, and they always got together with Sam and Sookie when they visited Sam's mom.

BERNADETTE MERLOTTE, Sam's mother, remarried eighteen months after the end of *Dead Ever After*. Her husband, a coyote shifter named Fred, was respectful of Bernie and loved to go on runs with her at the full moon. They had a very good time together.

CRAIG and **DEIDRA LISLE MERLOTTE** became the subject of a television special about the difficulties of marrying into a family containing the shapeshifter gene (*When Mom's a Dog*). Their marriage barely survived the experience, but after Deidra graduated from nursing school and Craig advanced in the tech-support department of a huge accounting firm, things calmed down. They presented Bernie with a granddaughter three years later, and after that they had triplet boys.

SAM MERLOTTE emerged from his death-to-life experience a stronger and more focused man, and he worked hard at not only his marriage to Sookie Stackhouse but also his business. When he and Sookie were ready to retire, they sold the bar and took a grand vacation to Thailand.

FRANKLIN MOTT, despite being old and crafty, was hunted down in his daytime hiding place by a human woman he'd dumped. She succeeded in killing him, and by the time his friends rose that night, his house had been stripped of everything of value.

SARAH NEWLIN was the only remaining voice of the FotS while she was in jail, but the interviews became few and far between. When she was finally released, only two FotS diehards in their late sixties came to the prison to pick her up. She had contracted lupus while she was in prison, and eventually (her worsening symptoms going untreated) she perished. The FotS presence at her funeral would hardly crowd a phone booth.

Werepanther leader **CALVIN NORRIS** and **TANYA GRIS-SOM NORRIS** remained married until Tanya made the mistake of yelling at a teen panther who'd knocked down their mailbox. Under the stress, the boy changed unexpectedly and killed Tanya with one blow, though he went a little crazy after that. The coroner didn't know what to make of the body's condition, and no one was ever charged. The teen panther was shipped to another community, way out in Montana. Calvin was taken care of by the entire female population of Hotshot after that, in every possible way. He died with a houseful of people around him, and he was content.

Calvin's daughter, **TERRY NORRIS**, backed by her mother, Maryelizabeth, succeeded Calvin as the leader of the Hotshot panthers. She was the first of a line of female leaders.

ERIC NORTHMAN threw himself into his role as Freyda's consort. He was surprised to see that Quinn was planning the ceremony, but he played his part with great attention to detail. If his heart was not in the joining, no one knew it. Or expected it, for that matter. After a couple of years, Eric became genuinely attached to Freyda, who showed herself to be strong but fair. When Pam called Eric to tell him about a wedding in Bon Temps, Eric sat without speaking for a few minutes before asking Pam to send him a picture of the bride. When the picture arrived, Eric looked at it for half an hour, then tore it up and burned it. After that, Freyda never questioned his loyalty. Eric's pride and his own survival depended on his protecting his vampire wife's back and furthering her interests. Freyda came to rely on him more and more, and gradually Eric lost any inclination to pine for the past. After twenty years, he uncovered a plot against

Freyda and demolished the conspirators in a blood-bath that was spoken of with awe by vampires everywhere. He seemed happier after that. To celebrate their fiftieth anniversary, Freyda offered to release him from his second century of marriage, but Eric refused without an instant's pause. He did ask for the boon of creating another child. When Freyda graciously agreed, she was wise enough not to put any conditions on her gift, and in return Eric was wise enough not to change a woman. But the lucky young man was a blue-eyed blond.

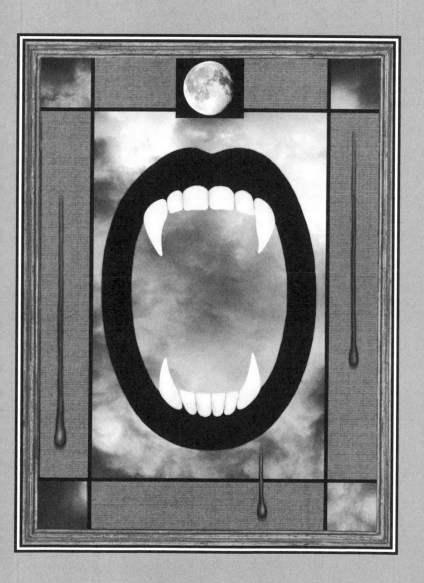

TOGO OLYMPIO continued to roam the Southwest. For years he dropped in to visit Trish and stayed with her for a few happy days . . . or weeks. As Trish got older, Togo's visits became longer, until one morning he woke to find she had passed. Togo left a note with her nearest neighbor and returned to his wanderings.

PALOMINO became a famous model due to her unusual coloring and her fabulous flexibility. When she grew tired of that, she returned to Louisiana during the reign of Bill Compton and handled the complaint department for his video game business.

PRESTON PARDLOE (his true fae name was Conor) was favored by Niall for many years. He is still well-known for his talent at gift giving.

DELL and **JANICE HERVEAUX PHILLIPS** were divorced three years after Dell dissed Sookie in Jackson. Janice married a really nice barber named Corky, and they had a wonderful time after they opened a huge salon together.

JOE PORTUGAL, the two-natured airman who died in the Witch Wars, attained status as a legend among young werewolves worldwide, possibly because of a photograph of him looking incredibly handsome and tough in the cockpit of an airplane.

LORINDA PRESCOTT continued to decorate her family home for every possible holiday, and she was featured in the Homes and Gardens section of the Bon Temps paper nearly every year.

DANNY PRIDEAUX was devastated after his breakup with Kennedy Keyes, but he managed to console himself with Hotshot's Terry Norris. After she'd had the obligatory two children with two different male panthers, she cleaved only to Danny. She makes him leave Hotshot every full moon when the panthers hunt together.

Wright ranch owner **TRISH GRAHAM PULASKI**, long-time lover of Togo Olympio, left all her property to the cause of abandoned animals. The SPCA in Wright was able to build a completely new facility, a no-kill shelter.

SELAH PUMPHREY was very successful with her real estate career in Little Rock, but she never forgot Bill or forgave him for not loving her. She had a rather unhappy life.

JAKE PURIFOY did not survive the bombing of the Pyramid of Gizeh in Rhodes.

Quinn's sister, **FRANNIE QUINN**, found her true love while she was waitressing, and they got married and stayed that way. She was relieved when her mother died and was glad to see her brother when he came to visit. She was just as glad to see him leave.

JOHN QUINN had many more adventures.

RASUL was recalled from his spying job in Michigan by Felipe when he finally remembered where Victor had sent Rasul. By that time, Rasul was reluctant to leave, so Felipe swapped him for one of the Michigan vampires.

SHERIFF PAM RAVENSCROFT continues to be a successful manager for Fangtasia and instituted such popular promotions as Wet Jock Night, Ladies Free Night, and Kiss a Vampire Night. The bar rakes in money, and Pam got a big raise from Felipe, which enabled her to have the kind of dream wedding with Heidi that she was sure Heidi wanted. They both wore white dresses. Pam remained fond of Sookie and visited her every so often . . . always by surprise.

When Felipe sold off Arkansas, his regent there, **RED RITA**, bought it. Red Rita saw potential in the state that no one else had recognized, and she's working hard to turn Arkansas into a destination state for vampire vacations. It is uphill work, but she's making progress.

SALOME's episode on the History Channel, part of the series *Undead History: Vampires Recall*, was the highest-rated hour of the season. She told her side of the story about the Dance of the Seven Veils, and to everyone's delight, she performed it. She had a great time. She even reenacted a minion bringing her the head of John the Baptist. When Sookie watched the episode, she thought the head looked a lot like that of the vampire Mickey.

ERIN and **REMY SAVOY** had one more child, a girl, Hope, after they married. When the economic climate improved, the family moved to Shreveport, where Erin worked for Home Depot and Remy as a carpenter for a home builder. As Remy reached fifty, he developed rheumatoid arthritis and gradually became unable to work. Erin was a little bitter at having to support the family, but their church was a big help, and she gradually became reconciled to his condition. Walking became difficult for Remy, and he was in a lot of pain. It was almost a relief when he caught pneumonia and passed away two days later. Erin remarried within eighteen months and had a happy second marriage.

HUNTER SAVOY was delighted when his dad married Erin, who didn't always understand him but always loved him. Hunter had a very hard time during his teen years, but he was lucky enough to have his "aunt" Sookie to visit with, and his cousins to play with, two of whom absolutely understood him. Hunter went into the military, and when his talents were discovered (despite his best efforts), he was added to an intelligence unit as an interrogator. His tremendous accuracy without any brutality made him one of the army's best-kept secrets, and he was loaned to the UK for some special questioning sessions. When he retired from the military after he'd served ten years, he had all kinds of medals and commendations, none of which he ever showed anyone. He had many adventures after that.

MICHELE SCHUBERT was happy with Jason because she knew his limitations and demanded just enough of him. She was as loyal to him as he was to her, and she was a firm mother and an indulgent grandmother.

TV host and vampire **TODD SEABROOK** was totally freaked out after his throat was torn out on national television. He never recovered from that episode, sure he looked weak in the eyes of American vampires after the incident. He stuck with *The Best Dressed Vamp* for the rest of the season, but then he retired to live by himself in a mountain valley in Colorado, where he feeds on sheep and whatever other game he can hunt.

DELIA SHURTLIFF continued to run contractor **RANDALL SHURTLIFF**'s life until they both went into an assisted-living center. The only person who seemed to mind was his first wife, Mary Helen, who continued to plague them until her three children put her into a different nursing home, miles away.

EVERETT O'DELL SMITH graduated from Tulane, and with a high recommendation from Mr. Cataliades, he was hired at a prestigious investment firm in New Orleans. Everett worked his way up through the ranks, slowly but steadily, finally achieving a partnership. He married late and wisely and had one daughter who could afford to work for a nonprofit charity to aid high-achieving kids from low-income families.

DR. SONNTAG married her diving instructor after a scuba vacation in Florida.

JASON STACKHOUSE had a surprisingly good marriage. To everyone's amazement except Michele's, he never cheated on her. Michele stayed on at her ex-father-in-law's car dealership until she retired, though the dealership had long since passed into other hands. Jason kept his job with the parish. After miscarrying once, Michele bore two children, Marie and Corbett. Marie was sweet natured and telepathic (that damn essential spark), but not too bright, and the combination led to Marie's having many problems in school, though she inherited the Stackhouse good looks. Corbett, a year younger, spent a lot of his school years defending his sister. When she graduated from high school and started working at a dog food factory, it was a big relief for Corbett, who got a football scholarship to go to college. Sadly, bitten werepanther Jason suddenly collapsed and died while he was in his parish truck supervising a work crew, at age fifty-five. Michele said being married twice was enough for her, and she never tried it again. Marie had a baby out of wedlock who was two years old when Marie married Jason Fortenberry, who was no rocket scientist himself. Corbett hit the marriage jackpot with the daughter of a very rich lawyer. Corbett became a private investigator working almost exclusively for his father-in-law's firm, though he did some divorce work to pay the bills.

SOOKIE STACKHOUSE married Sam in December, but a year later than Sookie had imagined. They really did take their time, and by their wedding day they were as sure as any two people could be that they were suited to each other. The entire Merlotte family attended the wedding, and of course so did Jason and Michele, Remy and Erin and Hunter, Alcide Herveaux, Mustapha Khan and Warren, Hoyt and Holly, and many other friends from Bon Temps and Wright. Though Sam had attended the fundamentalist church in Clarice for a few months, they opted for Sookie's Methodist church for the wedding and attended it thereafter, though not every Sunday. They discussed having the wedding at night so their vampire acquaintances could attend, but instead chose to have it in the day. (Pam threw them a party at Fangtasia on a night soon afterward. Weirdly, it was Thalia's idea.)

Sookie wore white because it was traditional and

she looked good in white, what with her tan and all. Sam wore a suit. Sam's brother, Craig, was his best man, and Tara was Sookie's matron of honor.

Sookie was startled to get a wedding gift from Eric, a very expensive and very impersonal silver flatware setting for twelve in a simple and elegant design. It took her an hour to write a thank-you note. Pam delivered the gift, at the same time requesting that Sookie wear her wedding dress to the vampire reception at Fangtasia. Heidi took several photographs at the reception, and Sookie suspected who would be looking at them.

Sookie was quite proud of her silver service and hauled it out on holidays for years. One morning after the wedding, Sookie found a rose blooming in her backyard—in December—with an envelope attached. Niall gave the couple an invitation to the Summerlands when they "went through the human veil," as Niall put it. They've put that in their lockbox at the bank.

Sookie and Sam had four children, the last being a complete surprise. Neal and Jennings came first, followed by Adele and their "bonus baby," Jillian Tara.

Though comfortable financially, Sookie and Sam wanted to be sure they could put four kids through college, so they started renting the bar for wedding receptions, and with Antoine's successor's help, they began to cater parties. All four of the kids worked as teenagers, since Sookie was determined they'd all learn how to be self-sufficient. This led to some yelling matches with the girls, especially when their mom's rare but impressive temper came into play. Jennings, to Sookie's dismay, inherited the family "disability." Mr. Cataliades showed up after each birth, though Sookie certainly never told him when she'd had a baby. He did tell Sookie that after this generation, his favor to his friend could be retired, and Sookie said, "Thank God."

At least Jennings, Marie, and the somewhat older Hunter had each other to talk to and commiserate with, though it was impossible for them to play games together.

All the Merlotte children grew up tolerant, since they all knew their dad was a shapeshifter and Uncle Jason a werepanther. The children also learned to accept vampires but to remain very wary in their presence. They thought "Aunt" Pam was hysterically funny. Go figure.

Sookie and Sam are still happier than many other couples because they talk about their feelings and they are great with compromise. Sam looks a little tense when Eric is on television, and for a while he wasn't too happy when Bill came over to visit, but gradually he became secure in Sookie's love and loyalty.

They're still thinking about Niall's offer, but not too seriously.

Vampire **THALIA** had such a fan following that she finally refused to come to Fangtasia any longer because people wanted to talk to her and have their pictures taken with her. Bill taught her how to blog. *Thalia's Thoughts* was a huge success in Internet terms, and Thalia actually enjoys writing about how inconsistent and ridiculous humans are. She was asked to endorse high-end security systems and an online dating club for opinionated supernaturals. She enjoys testing the security systems, but her dates have a way of vanishing.

DAVID and **GENEVIEVE THRASH** finally tracked down Sookie years after she'd warned them in time to escape disaster at Sophie-Anne's party house in New Orleans. After they reconnected with her, there were never any problems with Merlotte's state licenses.

TIJGERIN, Quinn's mate—at least for a time—persisted in her plan of birthing and raising her child in secrecy. She did keep Quinn up-to-date. They had a boy named Diederik.

The weather witch **JULIAN TROUT** disappeared from Channel 7 in Rhodes (and the supernatural scene) with his wife, Olive, following his realization that he could have saved lives in New Orleans by predicting the severity of Katrina . . . if anyone besides supernaturals would have listened to him. It took years for Trout to come to terms with his conscience. After that, he got a job at the Weather Channel, where he does his best to avert disasters.

Barmaid **INDIA UNGER** drove up to Iowa with physical therapist Gwen Long to get legally married. They adopted a child, a baby boy with a cleft palate. He had a few surgeries, but he became a handsome young man. India kept her job at Merlotte's until she began working at a Denny's and eventually became the manager. She and Gwen had a few bumps in the road facing homophobia and racism, but they remained together. Their son became a hospital administrator.

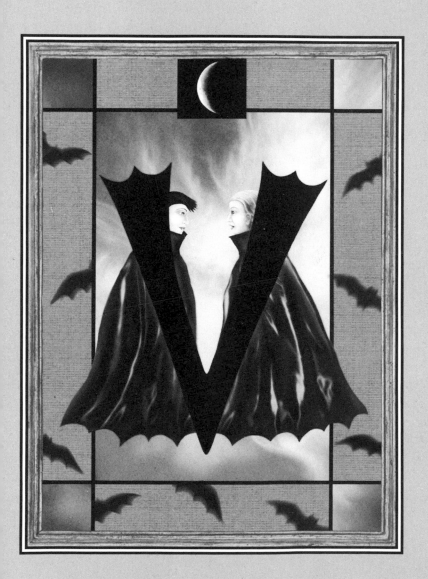

JUDITH VARDAMON continued to drop in on Bill every ten years or so, to "see how he was doing." Sadly, he never found it in him to return her affection.

Texas vampire **JOSEPH VELASQUEZ** kept his position as King of Texas for the next two hundred years. He never trusted a human telepath again.

GLEN and **PORTIA BELLEFLEUR VICK** had a son, Matthew, who was a total nerd and proud of it. He inherited his dad's skill with numbers and his mother's calm perseverance, and he became a lawyer with a practice focusing on estate planning. When he was in his midthirties, he married a very nice interior decorator named Jonathan.

WARREN continued to be a great marksman and constant companion of Mustapha Khan's for many years, though he never fully recovered from his ordeal at the hands of Jannalynn.

FBI agent **SARA WEISS** resigned in the year following her shooting. She became a follower of all things supernatural. Her husband and sons didn't know what to make of this development, and Sara grew more and more despondent as they drifted further apart. She got a job as a firearms instructor at a local gun range and finally began to put her life back together.

QUIANA WONG drifted down to New Orleans after her apprenticeship with Marilyn to make her own living as a psychic. She'd learned how to make a public splash and emphasized her Asian heritage by wearing a kimono and a fantastic hairdo. Backed by some seed money from Amelia Broadway, eventually Quiana opened a store called The World of Wong, with a stable of psychic readers, "magic" objects and books, and a huge inventory of kimonos.

XAVIER, the bouncer at Stompin' Sally's, recovered slowly from his wound. He trained with an old army buddy to get back in shape, and eventually he resumed his job at the country-and-western bar. He and Sally grew close during his recuperation, and though they didn't marry, they lived together for the rest of their lives.

VERENA ROSE YANCY established a scholarship in honor of her murdered daughter, Adabelle. Ostensibly, the scholarship pays for the education of any young woman interested in fashion and merchandising, provided she passes the examination of Verena's lawyer. In actuality, the young woman most like to be chosen is a werewolf.

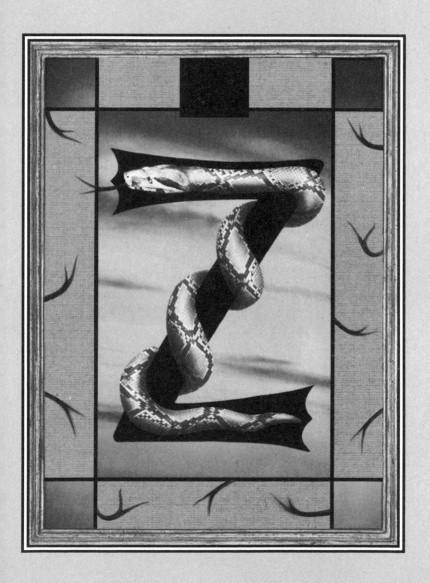

BETHANY ZANELLI, coach of the Lady Falcons (and wife of Chet Zanelli), had twin girls during her fifth year in Bon Temps. She was offered a job with a big high school in Missouri, but her mother was getting old, so Coach Zanelli stayed in Bon Temps to take care of her. She never regretted it.